THAT SAME FLOWER

THAT SAME FLOWER

Floria Aemilia's Letter
to Saint Augustine

JOSTEIN GAARDER

Translated by Anne Born

Farrar · Straus · Giroux

New York

Farrar, Straus and Giroux
19 Union Square West, New York 10003

Copyright © 1996 by H. Aschehoug & Co. (W. Nygaard), Oslo
Translation copyright © 1998 by Anne Born
All rights reserved
Distributed in Canada by Douglas & McIntyre Ltd.
Printed in the United States of America
Designed by Jonathan D. Lippincott
First published in 1996 by H. Aschehoug & Co.
(W. Nygaard), Norway, as *Vita Brevis*
First Farrar, Straus and Giroux edition, 1998

Library of Congress Cataloging-in-Publication Data
Gaarder, Jostein, 1952–
    [Vita brevis. English]
    That same flower / Jostein Gaarder ; translated
    by Anne Born.
        p.   cm.
    ISBN 0-374-25384-6 (alk. paper)
    I. Born, Anne.   II. Title.
    PT8951.17.A17V5813   1998
    839.8'2374—dc21   97-26681

THAT SAME FLOWER

When I visited the book fair in Buenos Aires in the spring of 1995, I was urged to set aside a morning for the renowned flea market in San Telmo. After a few hectic hours in front of all the stalls on streets and marketplaces, I ended up taking refuge in a small anti-quarian bookshop. Amid a modest selection of old manuscripts was a red file box la-beled Codex Floriae. *Something must have aroused my interest, because I opened the* box carefully and looked down at a bundle of handwritten sheets. They were certainly old—extremely old—and I quickly realized that the text was in Latin.

An introductory greeting was written in large letters on a single line: FLORIA AEMILIA AURELIO AUGUSTINO EPISCOPO HIPPONIENSI SALUTEM. *Greetings from Floria Aemilia to Aurelius Augustine, Bishop of Hippo . . . So it must be a letter. But could it really be written to the theologian and church father who from the middle of the fourth century onward spent most of his life in North Africa? From someone who called herself Floria?*

I was already well acquainted with Augustine's biography. No other single figure demonstrates more clearly the dramatic transition from the old Greco-Roman culture to the universal Christian one that was to characterize Europe right up to our own time. The best source of Augustine's life is, naturally, Augustine himself. Through his Confessions (Confessiones, c. A.D. 400) he provides a unique insight into both the turbulent fourth century in general and his own spiritual conflicts relating to faith and doubt. Augustine is probably the pre-Renaissance individual closest to ourselves.

Who was the woman who could have written a long letter to him? For the box held at least seventy or eighty sheets. I had never heard of any such document.

I tried to translate another sentence. "As a matter of fact, it seems odd to address you in this manner. Once, long, long ago, I would merely have written to 'My playful little Aurel.'" I couldn't be quite certain *about the translation, but that the letter was of a very personal nature I had no doubt.*

Then something struck me. Could the letter in the red file box possibly be from Augustine's longtime concubine, and therefore from the woman he had had to renounce, as he himself writes, because he had elected to spend the rest of his life abstaining from all sensual love? I felt a chill down my back, because I was aware that the Augustinian tradition knows no more about either the unfortunate woman or her many years of cohabiting with Augustine than the account he himself gives in the Confessions.

Soon the proprietor of the bookshop was beside me, pointing down at the box. I was still spellbound by the manuscript I had been trying to decipher.

"Really something," he said.

"Yes, I guess so . . ."

There had already been some interviews of me in newspapers and on television in connection with the book fair, so he recognized me.

"El mundo de Sofía?"

I nodded. Then he bent over the box, closed it, and placed it neatly on top of a small pile of manuscripts, as if to emphasize that he was not exactly burning to sell this one. Maybe he was slightly more doubtful since he now knew who I was.

"A letter to Saint Augustine?" I asked.

I thought he smiled uneasily.

"And you believe it's genuine?"

He replied, "It's not impossible. But I've only had it for a few hours, and if I knew for sure that this document is what it purports to be, it wouldn't be lying here."

"How did you get hold of it?"

He laughed. "I wouldn't have lasted very long in this business if I hadn't learned to protect my clients."

I was beginning to feel a kind of impatience and said, "How much are you asking for it?"

"Fifteen thousand pesos."

Fifteen thousand! That was like a punch in the side. The manuscript could certainly be several hundred years old, and it did profess to be a letter from Augustine's concubine. But at best we were probably talking about a transcript of a hitherto unknown letter to the church father, or, more likely, a copy of an even older transcript.

Of course it could just as well have been written in a Latin-American monastery sometime during the seventeenth or eigh-

teenth century. Even that would be quite something to take back to Europe. I thought I'd heard that in certain religious communities this kind of apocryphal letter was written to or from Catholic saints now and again.

The shopkeeper began closing up, and I passed him my credit card.

"Twelve thousand pesos," I said.

It was just over twelve thousand dollars —for something that might not have any antiquarian value whatsoever. But I was curious, and I wasn't the first person to pay dearly for his curiosity. Even when I initially read Augustine's Confessions many years earlier, I had tried to put myself in the place of this concubine. And Augustine's view of the love between man and woman has been extremely influential since the fifth century.

The bookseller accepted my offer. He said, "I think we'd be wisest to regard this transaction as a kind of risk-spreading."

I shook my head, not understanding what he meant.

He explained: "Either I'm making an extremely good deal or you're making an even better one." He separated the credit card slip and said regretfully: "I haven't even managed to read the manuscript myself. In a few days either the price would have doubled or I would have tossed the box into that basket you see over there."

I glanced at the basket he indicated. It was full of old paperbacks. A sign sticking out of it said: 2 PESOS.

———

It was I who made the best deal. The Codex Floriae *has now been dated to the end of the sixteenth century and was most probably penned in Argentina. The big question is whether it was really transcribed from an old parchment.*

I myself am no longer in any doubt about the authenticity of the letter, or about the fact that it must be attributed to Augustine's lover of many years. I think it is almost impossible to imagine that it was fabricated in Argentina toward the end of the sixteenth century. So in spite of everything, it is simpler to assume that the letter really did originate in Augustine's time. Both the syntax and the vocabulary are as if carved out of late antiquity, as is Floria's blend of sensuality and almost religious reflection.

In the fall of 1995 I took the manuscript to the Vatican Library in Rome for a more accurate analysis. But I was offered little help there. On the contrary: the Vatican continues to claim that it has never received any Codex Floriae. *This doesn't surprise me, although I can't just accept that Floria's letter belongs to the Catholic church.*

I had naturally made sure to photocopy the manuscript, and during the spring of 1996 I attempted to garb the letter in Norwegian dress. Where the letter cites Augustine's Confessions, *though, I chose to resort to Oddmund Hjelde's outstanding Norwegian translation of the first ten books.*

The work of translation has been a jigsaw puzzle without parallel, not least because Floria's manuscript has no pagination. At the same time it has been immensely stimulating to have this opportunity to brush up on my old facility in Latin—acquired long ago at Oslo Cathedral School (1968–71). I have sent many grateful thoughts to my old Latin teacher, Oskar Fjeld.

It is fascinating how old conjugations and declensions remain as if nailed to the memory. Nevertheless, without the benevolent assistance of Øivind Andersen this translation would not have been possible. Thanks also to Trond Berg Eriksen, Egil Kraggerud, Øivind Norderval, and Kari Vogt for encouraging words and good advice.

Nothing would please me more than if this edition of the Codex Floriae were rewarded by a renewed interest in the Latin language and in classical culture as a whole.

I

Greetings from Floria Aemilia to Aurelius Augustine, Bishop of Hippo.

As a matter of fact, it seems odd to address you in this manner. Once, long, long ago, I would merely have written to "My playful little Aurel." But now, more than ten years have passed since you put your arms around me, and much has changed.

I write because the priest of Carthage has allowed me to read your confessions. He thought your books might be edifying reading for a woman like me. As a catechumen[1] I've belonged in a way to the congregation here for many years already, but I shall not allow myself to be baptized, Aurel. It is not the Nazarene who stands in my way, nor is it the four gospels; but I shall not be baptized.

In Book VI you write: "The woman I lived with was not permitted to stay at my side. They took her away because she was a hindrance to my forthcoming marriage. My heart, which was deeply attached to her, was pierced, and wounded so that it bled. She returned to Africa and promised you[2] she

[1] I.e., listener. Floria uses the Latin word *auditor*.

[2] I.e., God. *Confessions* was written as Augustine's confessions to God.

would never have anything to do with another man. She left our natural son with
me."[3]

It is good to see you can still remember
how closely bound we once were to each
other. You know our union was something
more than the kind of fleeting cohabitation
customary before the man marries. We lived
faithfully together for over twelve years and
had a son together. People we met often took
us to be man and wife according to the law.
And you liked that, Aurel. I think it made
you a little proud, for many men are
ashamed of their wives. Can you remember
when we crossed the bridge over the Arno
River? Suddenly you just stopped me with a

[3] *Conf.* VI, 15.

hand on my shoulder. Then you said something. Do you remember?

Several times you say that you are leaving out many things and that you have forgotten a great deal. You must forgive me if I help you on one or two important points.

It is true that I promised not to know any other man. But I did not make that vow to God. Wasn't it *you* who begged me to make that vow? I am sure about this, for it was my only consolation when I traveled home alone from Milano.[4] You still cared—a little, anyway—about me. And perhaps Monica[5] would change her mind, perhaps we two would put our arms around each other again.

---

[4] Floria uses the Latin name *Mediolanum*.

[5] Augustine's mother.

For one doesn't ask for fidelity from a person one rejects in hatred or anger. A little further on you write: "My wound, inflicted when my relationship with the woman I lived with was brought to an end, would not heal either. At first it was inflamed and terribly painful, but then it festered, and I grew less sensitive to pain."[6] Ah, well, I shall return to that sensitivity and pain, and to the festering.

As we both know, I wasn't torn away from you just because Monica had found a suitable girl. Naturally that was Monica's reasoning: she was thinking of the future of the family. Or was she a little jealous of me, too? That was something I often wondered about. I can't forget that spring when she came

[6] *Conf.* VI, 15.

sweeping into Milano and somehow put herself between us.

But it was the two of you who sent me away. And for you it was not chiefly on account of the planned marriage but for another reason as well. You thrust me from you because you loved me too much, you said. It's normal, of course, to stand by a loving partner. But you did the opposite thing, because you had already started to disdain passionate love between man and woman. You thought I bound you to the world of the senses, leaving you no peace and quiet in which to concentrate on the salvation of your soul. As a consequence, nothing came of that proposed marriage either. God desires above all that man should live in abstinence, you write. I have no faith in such a God.

What unfaithfulness, Aurel! What a sublime betrayal you were guilty of when you sent me away! In your heart you cleaved to me, and your heart was wounded so that it bled. My heart suffered the same hurt, naturally, if that signifies anything, for we were two souls torn from each other, or two bodies, if you wish; or, in fact, two souls in one body. Your wound would not heal: it was inflamed and terribly painful until eventually it festered and you grew less sensitive to the pain. But why? Well, because you loved the salvation of your own soul more than you loved me. What times, Esteemed Bishop, what manners![7]

---

[7] *O tempora, o mores!* Cicero makes use of the expression several times in his orations. With her constant allusions to Roman writers and philosophers, Floria may wish to emphasize that she is now a well-read woman.

Have you never thought through what happened? Judging by your confessions, I think not. But isn't it precisely an intensified form of infidelity to desert one's beloved for the sake of saving one's own soul? Wouldn't it be easier for a woman to bear if the man left her because he wanted to marry—or because he preferred another woman, for that matter? But there was no other woman in your life. You merely loved your own soul more than me. Your own soul, Aurel, that was what you wanted to rescue, that which had once found rest in me. You never had any particular desire to get married, as long as I was by your side, you said. This marriage Monica arranged was merely a filial duty. And you never did marry. Your bride was not of this world.

Then there was our son and, as God is my

witness, I was as much mother of Adeodatus as you were his blood father. It was I who bore him, and it was I who nursed him at my breast, for we had no wet nurse. Then I left him with you, as you say. No mother does this willingly, no mother deserts her only son without suffering the most agonizing grief. But without you beside me I could make no demands, for I had no fortune. Wasn't that why Monica wanted to have you married to a girl of high rank? I think it was a Greek who said that justice exists only among equals.[8]

In Book IX you beseech God to accept your confessions also for the innumerable

---

[8] I have been unable to discover which Greek writer Floria refers to.

things you pass over in silence. One of these omissions is our last meeting, and perhaps that is what you have in mind, for you say not a word about what you did in Roma for a whole year before you came back to Africa. When you make such a great effort to write down your confessions, I think this omission is almost shameful.

What do you think now about what happened in Roma? How could it happen to us, Aurel? Perhaps it was actually in that wretched room up on the Aventine that your spiritual soul-searching was to begin. I am sure you heard I had managed to get to Ostia more or less safe and sound. There I obtained passage almost at once, and the voyage itself, considering the circumstances, went well— at least I arrived back in Carthage. This time, too, it was you who paid for the journey. It was the second time I was sent back to Africa, almost like a piece of merchandise. It is long ago now, and the wounds have healed.

Ever since I came back from Milano almost fifteen years ago, I have walked in your footsteps. Or perhaps I should say I have retraced our old paths in Carthage. First I read everything I could get hold of on philosophy. For I had to find out what there was in philosophy that could divide a loving pair. If you had become attached to another woman I might have wanted to see her. But my rival was not another woman I could see with the naked eye, she was a philosophical principle. So in order to understand you better I had to go some way along the same road you had taken. I had to read philosophy.

My rival was not only *my* rival. She was every woman's rival, she was love's own angel of death.[9] You yourself refer to her as Abstinence. Book VIII, Aurel! You write: "Then I was given to see abstinence in her pure beauty, serene and cheerful, but without frivolity in her joy. With appealing friendliness she bade me come without hesitation. Then she stretched out her pious hands to receive and embrace me."[10]

Here you say a great deal in very few words![11] You do not even try to conceal how you allowed yourself to be seduced. I cannot deny that my heart seethed with jeal-

[9] *Obitus veneris*, i.e., "the annihilation of love."

[10] *Conf.* VIII, 11.

[11] *Multa paucis.*

ousy when I read that particular section. For wasn't it in somewhat the same fashion that you gave yourself to me when we were aglow with youth? Wasn't it with "appealing friendliness" that I tried to embrace you? I feel like saying with Horace: When foolish people want to avoid making a mistake, they usually do the opposite thing![12]

I began with Cicero[13] as you did. In Book III you write about him: "But there was one thing in particular I loved in Cicero's exhortation: it spurred me not to seek this or that

[12] *Dum vitant stulti vitia in contraria currunt.*

[13] Cicero (106–43 B.C.), Roman statesman, orator, and philosopher, was instrumental in spreading the knowledge of Greek philosophy in Rome. As a philosopher he can most accurately be characterized as an eclectic, i.e., one who seeks to fuse the best of various philosophical systems. *Hortensius*, the text to which Augustine refers in *Confessions*, is now lost.

philosophical direction but to love and seek and win truth itself . . ."[14] And truth, Aurel, is what has spurred me to read the philosophers and the great poets. I have read the four gospels as well. Since we were torn apart, I have devoted my life totally to truth[15]—as you once set out to devote yourself to abstinence. You are still dear to me, although I must add that today truth is still more dear.[16] Now I am considered a learned woman and I give private lessons here in Carthage. Don't you think that's quite amusing, by the way

[14] *Conf.* III, 4.

[15] Floria is playing on an expression taken from the satires of Juvenal (*Vitam impendere vero*).

[16] A play on the following statement, according to tradition derived from Aristotle: *Amicus Plato, sed magis amica veritas* (Plato is dear to me, but truth is still more dear).

—that now it is I who am the teacher of rhetoric? Or have you lost your sense of humor, too? There isn't much humor in your confessions, Aurel. It was different for the two of us. We could laugh and joke from sunset to sunrise. Today you'd probably say humor is the same as sensual passion or self-indulgence.

All the same, I must thank you for your books. No other writings[17] have given me more insight into why you first wanted to leave me to wait for an eleven-year-old girl to become old enough to marry you—and then you later chose to worship the goddess you call Abstinence. I am grateful that you

---

[17] I imagine that here Floria is thinking of philosophical writings by other authors.

write so frankly and sincerely. That your memory can play tricks on you now and then is quite another matter, and this is one of the reasons for my letter. Tacitus wrote that it is fitting for women to grieve over a loss, for men to remember it.[18] But you don't even remember, Aurel!

I have three letters in front of me. You sent one of them from Milano soon after deciding not to get married after all. Not many months had passed since I had been forced to leave. Then I received your letter from Ostia when Monica died. How sweet of you to allow Adeodatus to add a little message to his mother. A year or two later I had another letter. It was after the poor boy was taken

---

[18] *Feminis lugere honestum est, viris meminisse.*

from you. Did anyone see you weep then? For certainly you don't believe the boy fell sick and died because he was conceived in sin? The reason I ask this is because of something you write in Book IX. Here you refer to Adeodatus as "the fruit of my sin." True, you add that God "has the power to make something beautiful out of our abomination."[19] For you had no other part in the boy than sin, you write. You should be ashamed of yourself, Aurel, you who named him Adeodatus![20] Surely you don't believe the Lord did away with the boy to help you in your career as priest and bishop? May he look mercifully upon your delusions!

A son dies, Aurel. I think you should have

[19] *Conf.* IX, 6.

[20] He who is given by God.

come to me so we could have wept a little together, you and I. You were not yet ordained, nor were you betrothed, and Adeodatus was our only son. But perhaps you were so full of shame for what had happened in Roma that you didn't have the courage to meet me? Or were you afraid the same thing might happen again?

I don't really understand why it has become so difficult for you to weep. Book IX, Aurel! Do you really think it is too carnal a thing to show grief? You would not even allow your own son to let his tears flow freely when he had to bid farewell to his grandmother! I think it must be more "carnal" to hold back the tears, for when we do not have a good cry the grief will often stay inside us like a heavy burden. Peace be with the boy's memory!

As I mentioned, I was able to borrow your confessions from the priest here in Carthage. Forgive me for copying out some sections that I shall comment on further. I hope you have the patience to read my reflections with an open mind. Or my confessions, if you like. For I regard this letter as something more than a personal greeting from me to you: it is also a letter to the Bishop of Hippo Regius. Years have passed, and much has changed since we two embraced each other.

Thus what I write might equally be a letter to the whole Christian church, because today you are a man of great influence.

I must admit that this very thought alarms me, but I pray to God that a woman's voice too may be heard by men of the church. Perhaps you recall something I said to you that morning we walked down to the Forum Romanum and saw the thin layer of snow covering the Palatine. I talked of Seneca's tragedy *Medea*, which I had just read. In the play he says that the other side should also be heard, and the other side was me.[21]

---

[21] Although Seneca does say one should listen to the other side, in Floria's letter this is differently phrased. Here this dialectical principle is formulated exactly as it was transmitted through Augustine's words *audiatur et altera pars* in his text *De duabus animabus*, from 391. Floria may have known this work. I myself prefer to meditate on the possibility that it is Augustine who in *De duabus animabus* expresses himself in the words Floria used at the Roman Forum in the winter of 388.

The first book begins so promisingly as you praise God for his wisdom and grandeur. "For of you, and through you, and in you are all things," you write.[22] Then you talk about your early childhood, although I think you borrow many of your observations from Adeodatus' first years. But already we find here the somber undertone that runs like a red thread through all your books: "To you, no one is pure and free from sin, not even the infant who lives but one day on earth . . . the helpless infant limbs may be innocent, but not the infant soul." And why not? Well, because you have seen a little boy who, "white with fury and with a spiteful expression," looked over at his brother who also

---

[22] *Conf.* I, 2. Cf. Romans 11:36.

wanted the breast. Poor Aurel! The child's desire for the breast does not make him evil! And you write, too, that God has "endowed the body with senses and limbs, adorned it with a beautiful form, and implanted in it all the instincts that will sustain and defend life."[23] But you do not dwell on this as something beautiful and good. Straightaway you start fretting again about being born in iniquity and your mother conceiving you in sin. But it was love, Honored Bishop, the child is conceived in love. God ordained the world so beautifully and wisely, he did not allow it to happen by germination.

You even think you can discern a deeper meaning in the fact that Monica did not have

[23] *Conf.* I, 7.

you baptized as a child. "For those spots of sin one contracted after the bath of baptism would certainly bring with them greater and more dangerous guilt."[24] Sin and guilt—because God created us man and woman with a rich register of senses and needs. Or with instincts, if you will, or titillating desires, Aurel—I can speak frankly to you, who once were my little itchy-fingered bedfellow. Even your youthful predilection for the story of Dido and Aeneas is added to your lifelong list of sins.

You write like this about "sensual lust" and "sinful desires" throughout all your books. Has it occurred to you that it might be you who look on God's gifts with scorn?

[24] *Conf.* I, 11.

It strikes me that your lack of regard for the world of the senses may derive from the Manichaeans[25] and the Platonists rather than from the Nazarene himself.

In Book X you are unreserved in emphasizing your contempt not only for the world of the senses, and thus for God's work of creation, but for the senses themselves—which also are God's work of creation, I would think. "The temptations of the sense of smell do not greatly appeal to me. When they are absent, I do not seek them; if they are present, I do not disdain them, but am

[25] Manichaeanism was a religious movement that had great influence in Augustine's time. Its half-religious, half-philosophical doctrine of salvation was based on the dualistic idea that the world is divided into good and evil, light and dark, spirit and matter. Man could rise above the material world with the aid of the spirit and thus lay the foundation for the soul's salvation.

prepared to go without them forever."[26] You are even ashamed when you sometimes catch yourself eating food because it tastes good. But now God has taught you "to use nourishment in the same way as one takes medicine." I congratulate you[27]—although the mere thought is nauseating to me. "Even when we eat for the sake of our health, a dangerous feeling of well-being is at our heels," you write. So it is "not always easy to know whether it is the necessary consideration for the sustenance of the body, or the deceptive desire for pleasure that demands service."[28] No, alas, Bishop, for what if some-

[26] Conf. X, 32.

[27] *Plaudite!* I.e., "Congratulations!"

[28] *Conf.* X, 31.

thing is both good for the gullet and healthy for the body at one and the same time! I myself turn to these simple words of Horace, and I do it with the best conscience in the world: "It is comforting to let oneself go now and again."[29]

You have to eat, Aurel, and you are permitted to enjoy your food. You have not given up washing as well? When you see a lovely flower, you may feel free to go and smell it—even if today you call that "the desire of the body." You should be ashamed of yourself. But "nothing is so absurd that it cannot have been said by a philosopher," writes Cicero.[30] The same thing could quite

[29] *Dulce est desipere in loco.*

[30] *Nihil tam absurdum dici potest ut non dicatur a philosopho.*

certainly be said of the theologians. Do you remember when we walked together over the Arno River? On the bridge you suddenly stopped because you wanted to smell my hair. Why did you want to do that, Aurel? Was it "the desire of the body" making itself felt again? I do not believe that; no, I believe you once knew what real love was, but now I am afraid you have forgotten.

In Book II you write about your youthful years in Tagaste, when your "soul was corrupted by sensual lust."[31] You write: "The chief thing that gave me pleasure was loving and being loved . . . But from the mire of physical desire and from the source of

[31] *Conf.* II, 1.

youthful urges murky vapors rose and left my heart in darkness and fog so that I could not distinguish between pure love and impure lust. Both feelings raced within me in blended confusion and dragged me, unsteady youth, down into an abyss of passions and pulled me under into a maelstrom of vices."[32]

I think you brag a little, Aurel. Like most young men you certainly had a lively imagination, but when I met you some years later it was a rather fumbling and inexperienced fellow I shared a bed with. You write, too, that you were ashamed not to have had as much experience as your companions maintained they had. They boasted of their

---

[32] *Conf.* II, 2.

"shameful vices," you say, so you did the same thing yourself. Yes, that sort of thing is childish, don't you agree? But shameful? Perhaps the most shameful thing of all is that the Bishop of Hippo Regius is still preoccupied with such childish pranks. A bishop should not find any human manifestation strange,[33] and boys will be boys, they always have been. You aren't even averse to mentioning that frightful "crime" you committed in your sixteenth year when, with a couple of other boys, you stole some fruit from a pear tree.[34]

Then you suddenly grow more serious.

[33] Play on the well-known quotation from Terence: *Homo sum; nihil humanum a me alienum puto* (I am a man: nothing human is alien to me).

[34] *Conf.* II, 6.

First you refer to Paul's words about it being "good for a man not to touch a woman."[35] And, dear Aurel, why do you cite only this one verse? I think it is owing to something you have brought with you from the Manichaeans. Did you not learn at the school of rhetoric how dangerous it can be to detach a single sentence from its context? It is true that Paul writes that it can be good for a man not to touch a woman, but, he goes on, in order to avoid fornication every man should have his own wife and every woman her own husband. He emphasizes further that woman and man shall be one body and constantly give themselves to each other so that neither shall be tempted into unfaithfulness because

[35] *Conf.* II, 2.

43

they cannot manage to live in abstinence.[36]

The question is whether it is especially wise to believe that one can be redeemed from "sinful vices" by choosing Abstinence. Rather the opposite, if you ask me. Truth to tell, you seem more absorbed in that kind of thing than most men your age, although it is almost fifteen years since you threw yourself into the arms of Mother Abstinence. Oh well, you did suffer a rather sizable relapse, of course. If you drive nature out with a hayfork, it will still return again, writes Horace.[37] Unless you deal with it more severely, for here it comes: you write that it would

---

[36] Floria's indignation over Augustine's extracting this one verse from its context seems understandable. See 1 Corinthians 7:1–7.

[37] *Naturam expellas furca, tamen usque recurret.*

44

have been best if in your youth you had castrated yourself for the sake of the kingdom
of heaven.[38] Then you could have waited for
the embrace of God with a happier mind.
Poor Aurel! How ashamed you are of being a
man, you who were my little stallion. Even
now—and this is many years after you chose
Abstinence as your bride—even now you
pour out your heart to the Lord and complain
that you still miss a woman at your side. In
Book X, Bishop, you write: "But in my memory, which I have talked so much about now,

---

[38] *Conf.* II, 2. Cf. Matthew 19:12. This verse in Matthew inspired
a few early Christians to castrate themselves, among them the
church father Origen (185–254). In the Vulgate, the Latin translation of the Bible used by Augustine, the verse is translated thus:
*Sunt enim eunuchi qui de matris utero sic nati sunt; et sunt
eunuchi qui facti sunt ab hominibus; et sunt eunuchi qui se ipsos
castraverunt propter regnum caelorum; qui potest capere capiat.*

there still live images of these things that have lodged there from old habit. They force themselves upon me, not vividly, it is true, when I am awake; but in sleep they tempt me, not only to pleasure but to assent and to act upon them."[39]

I gather from these confessions that you have not yet castrated yourself. Can it even be that now and again you miss me? Can it be the memories of me and our old "habits" that come to you in your dreams? For you have certainly not done *that*, Aurel? You who were once my proud bedpost. Why couldn't you just as well have blinded yourself? Oedipus did.[40] Why couldn't you cut

[39] *Conf.* X, 30.

[40] From Sophocles' tragedy *Oedipus Rex*. When Oedipus finally realized he had killed his father (Laius) and married his mother (Jocasta), he gouged out his eyes with Jocasta's ornamental pin.

out your tongue? For I am sure you still long for my kisses.

I think that your sex too was in a way a sense organ. Wasn't it, Aurel? Anyway, you are the one who keeps on writing about "sensual lust" when what you have in mind is the delights of love. Or do you believe that your eyes and ears are more divinely created than your sex? Do you think some parts of the human body are less worthy to God than others? For instance, is your middle finger more neutral than your tongue? You used your finger too!

III

In Book III you write of the time you came to Carthage as a young student: "A vicious erotic life boiled around me on all sides, exactly like a witch's caldron. I was not yet in love, but I longed for love. I kept my desires hidden and felt irritated with myself because I had so little craving. Out of the need for love I searched for something I could love."[41]

[41] *Conf.* III, 1.

Then you found me. You had been in town only a year when we met. I myself was born here. We were both in our nineteenth year. I remember sitting beneath a fig tree with three or four students. You already knew one of them and came walking toward us. Squinting in the sun, I looked up at you. I must have done so in a captivating manner, for you held my gaze but glanced down at the ground irresolutely once or twice before searching for my eyes again. It almost felt as if we two had already lived a life together. I knew at once that I could come to love you heart and soul. Yet I could have neither feared nor dreamed that it would happen that same night, although if I had sensed it I might perhaps have done both at once.

It was not so strange that I was with students, but you noticed with some astonishment that I took part in the conversation as much as any of them. And that was one of the first things we talked about as soon as you and I were alone together. When we were with the students we discussed Virgil, then life and love in general. I seem to recall that you noted with considerable surprise how naturally I defended Dido's deed of love.[42] It was as if you asked me with your eyes whether a woman could really love a man so deeply that she would take her own life if she was betrayed.

---

[42] From Virgil's *Aeneid*. Aeneas drifts ashore at Carthage after a shipwreck and engages in a passionate love affair with Dido, its Queen. But Aeneas has a great task ahead of him. He frees himself from Dido's embraces and sets course for Italy to establish an extensive kingdom, later to become Rome. He does this without showing any pity for Dido or her tragic fate. Brokenhearted, she takes her own life.

I don't know whether it was because we talked of Dido and Aeneas that you then suddenly asked me if I had been to Roma. Anyway, I thought it was a strange question, very strange, for we two did not know each other, and yet you wanted to know if I had been to Roma. I think I interpreted it as a kind of courting, for you were quick to say you had not been there yourself but had planned to go one day. Since we had just been talking of Dido, it was as if by this question you made me into the Queen of Carthage herself, and since I had defended this legendary Queen so fervently it was almost as though you wanted to say that if only I were yours you would want me to go to Roma with you, and you would never let me suffer the same fate as she. At that time I did not know that many years later the two of us really would travel to Roma together. But it seemed somehow that Aeneas' leaving Carthage was where it all began. Perhaps I should add that it was here everything ended as well. Like Aeneas, you, too, had a mission which was greater and more important than love in Carthage.

At the end of our first meeting we were left sitting by ourselves under the fig tree. Even then I think there must have been something about the two of us that somehow frightened the others, something strong and close, as if we were invisible conspirators. Then you went back with me to my little room, and stayed the night. Eighteen months later we had a son, and we were inseparable until Monica or Abstinence tore us away from each other and left us both with bleeding wounds.

From the beginning, our life was firmly grounded in sensuality, for we certainly cultivated Venus together, at times were equally unstoppable. When I read your confessions today, though, I have the sad feeling that what you now call the sensual was the only thing that bound the two of us to each other. You seem to be overzealous where repentance and remorse for your earlier life are concerned, and thus for the time before you dedicated yourself wholly to Abstinence. Is it really God or is it just as much your own doubt and remorse you are trying to exorcise?

Perhaps it is precisely our deep friendship you are most ashamed of. There are many men who feel more ashamed of cultivating the friendship of a woman than of devoting themselves to a sensual love relationship with her. Then they are likely to blame the sensual love for their inability to develop any sincere friendship with a woman as well. Unfortunately, the more philosophically schooled they are, the more tangible this is; I attribute much of the fault to the Manichaeans and the Platonists. I think you looked at me in a new way after you read the *Phaedo*,[43] and it was no better after you read Porphyrius.[44] So many heads, Aurel, so many opinions![45] I did not suspect real trouble until you started calling me Eve, but that was not until we had gone to Milano. It was

[43] The *Phaedo*, a dialogue by Plato in which Socrates discusses the arguments for the immortality of the soul.

[44] Porphyrius (232–304), Neoplatonic philosopher, pupil of Plotinus.

[45] After Horace: *Quot capita, tot sensus.*

when you did whatever you could to gain admittance to the circle around Ambrosius.[46]

You yourself write that your soul was not strong and well at that time. "Covered with abscesses it threw itself into misery, desiring to ease its itch with sensual pleasures. But even these were not entirely without soul; otherwise I would never have loved them. I felt it was delightful both to love and to be loved, especially when I was able to possess the beloved bodily. Thus I soiled the deep springs of friendship with impure sensual lust, and dulled its clear radiance with a hellish allure."[47]

So you do not hide how deeply and fer-

[46] Ambrosius (339–397) held a high position in the service of the state before being appointed Bishop of Milan.

[47] *Conf.* III, 1.

vently you now despise Venus. She, Aurel, who herself was the jeweled bridge between our two lonely and fearful souls. But that is not all. Now you despise all other sensual joys, too. And more, more: you go on to despise the senses themselves. Truly, you have become a eunuch!

I do not understand how you can sweep away our secrets simply by calling them "sensual lust" or "the lust for pleasure." Well, I did not understand it before I read in Book X that today you despise all the senses and everything they offer of fruit and wine to our souls. But this is not all. You start boasting to God about how deeply you now realize that you despise the whole of his creation. You do this because of a "radiance" you say you have seen with your inner eye.

In any case, I shall not forget your playful hands and your witty repartee. I see you have lost your way among the theologians. What a miserable occupation! How can the small preside over the great? How can the work define the master? Indeed, how can the work determine that it shall stop functioning as a work?

We are created human beings, Aurel. And we are created man and woman. In his writings on age Cicero says something about the youth not wishing for the strength of the lion or the elephant. We should not try to live as something other than what we are. Would that not be to mock God? We are human beings, Aurel. We must first live, and then—yes—then we can philosophize.[48]

---

[48] *Primum esse, tum philosophari.*

Was I nothing more than a woman's body to you? You know that isn't true. And how can you distinguish between body and soul? Isn't that bungling God's work of creation? Oh yes, it certainly is, my own faithless tiger. When you clawed me with your sharp caresses, you were also tearing at my soul.

You describe friendship so beautifully in Book IV, but then, of course, it is only friendship with men you have in mind: "We talked and laughed together and were kind to one another. Sometimes we read well-written books; sometimes we joked with each other; sometimes we exchanged civilities. Occasionally we disagreed, but with no animosity, rather as when a man disagrees with himself. But that kind of rare difference of opinion merely served to spice the unanimity that generally prevailed. We taught one another and learned from one another. When some of us were absent, we longed for them almost painfully and welcomed them joyfully on their return. With these and similar signs the love of friends can pass from heart to heart, through facial expression, words and glances and a thousand friendly gestures. They were like sparks that set our souls on fire and fused the many into one."[49]

When I read that section I almost felt as if I'd been eaten up—or in some way both eaten up and regurgitated all at once. For weren't these words equally applicable to our friendship? We talked and laughed together and were kind to one another—from sunset

[49] *Conf.* IV, 8.

to sunrise. We sent each other little secret signals "from heart to heart, through facial expression, words and glances and a thousand friendly gestures." Now you take the best things from our life together and somehow dare to preserve them in memory by limiting them to friendship between men. You were not quite so larcenous at the time we met beneath the fig tree. Certainly you did have a lot of friends then, exceptionally many, in fact. But the love we two entertained for each other was of another kind, so I was never jealous of your male friends. Sparks were struck between us which not only set our souls on fire but also ignited our bodies.

You don't exactly neglect to confess your remorse for our sensual love. However, do not on that account forget that I was your best friend as well. For you sank so deep into the mire, you cultivated friendship with a woman. I was not merely a sentient skin.[50] Your greatest offense[51] then was not that you loved a woman in the flesh—in that respect you were neither better nor worse than most. Your most outrageous sin[52] was that you also loved Eve's soul.

If it were not because you entreated God so earnestly to examine your heart, I should not bother to remind you of these bygone things, for it is a long time since we two embraced each other. But it seems as if you let Truth ride like an untamed foal through your

[50] *Scortum*, "skin"; the word can also mean "prostitute, whore."

[51] *Delictum.*

[52] *Peccatum.*

confessions. And let it run, Aurel, let it run all the way home to me. It will find rest here, for I am the only one who knows it.

Perhaps there may be a God who knows us. If so, I am quite sure he has stored up all the goodness we two gave each other. And if he doesn't exist, my old twin soul, then there can be none in the whole universe who know each other better than you and I. For you gave me body and soul, just as I pledged myself body and soul to you. Where you were, I was, and where I was, there you wanted to be.[53] First a mother came between us, then came the Manichaeans and the Platonists, and finally you put the theologians and Abstinence between us. Thus in a way

[53] Here Floria paraphrases an old Roman marriage formula.

you traveled even further away from me than Aeneas had traveled from Dido. May God look mercifully on your errors.

Were you and I not two sides of a body that was fused—as a bridge joins two sides of a river into one body? Then a mighty divinity suddenly rises up from the river—or an abstract principle of Abstinence—that seems to sever the connection between one riverbank and the other? No, I do not believe in such a God, Your Grace. This is something I have discussed with the priest of Carthage many times. He knows that I once lived with a man, but not that it was you. So didn't it seem like something taken from a tragedy when suddenly he came to me one morning with your confessions? Or was it something you had suggested to him?

Can you still remember how you stroked me all over and seemed to tighten every bud before it opened? How you enjoyed plucking me! How you allowed yourself to be intoxicated by my perfumes! How you nourished yourself on my juices! And then you went away and sold me for the sake of your soul's salvation. What infidelity, Aurel, what guilt! No, I don't believe in a God who demands human sacrifices. I don't believe in a God who lays waste to a woman's life in order to save a man's soul.

IV

We soon moved with our little boy—he was just two—to Tagaste, your birthplace, where you began to teach rhetoric. Toward the end of Book III you write: "Incidentally, I leave out a great deal here, because I am in a hurry to get to the things which are most pressing for me to confess to you. I have also forgotten much."[54]

[54] *Conf.* III, 12.

But surely you haven't forgotten how hard it was for Monica to have you living in her house with Adeodatus and me? Already then I felt that you and Monica were bound together by ties that are not natural between mother and son. I had my own ideas about Monica's visions, you know. You write about her dream: "She was standing on a tree trunk. A young man came up to her, radiant with happiness, and he smiled at her as she stood there burdened with sorrow. He asked why she grieved and wept every day. As is usual with such visions, he did this to manifest something to her, not to question her. She replied that she was lamenting because I was lost. Then he begged her not to worry and urged her to pay heed, and she would come to see that where she was, there was I also.[55] And when she looked up, she could see that I stood beside her on the same tree trunk."[56]

You repeat this, Aurel, as if to make what you have on your mind even clearer: "Where you are, there he is also."[57] You and Monica then, mother and son on the same tree trunk. Perhaps it was chiefly religion that was alluded to here, although it looks now as though you are reading more into it. Should not a man leave his father and mother, live with a woman, and the two be-

[55] I.e., Augustine.

[56] *Conf.* III, 11.

[57] Cf. footnote 53. Many people in Augustine's time must have associated his expression "where you were, there I was" with the relationship of man and woman in marriage.

come one flesh? She placed herself between us, and it was she who finally won the battle. She certainly was a powerful woman, with great ambition for herself and her son.

But let us hasten on to Book IX. You write of your own grief when Monica died at Ostia: "It was as if my life were torn to shreds. For her life and mine had become one."[58]

But, Aurel! Have you no shame? Have you quite forgotten Oedipus and Jocasta?[59] Oh, well, he blinded himself, and you wish you had castrated yourself, perhaps it comes to the same thing. Poet's frenzy,[60] Aurel! Now

---

[58] *Conf.* IX, 12.

[59] Cf. footnote 40. Unaware of what he is doing, Oedipus marries his own mother, with whom he has four children.

[60] *Furor poeticus*, i.e., "poetic frenzy."

and again it's tempting to tell the truth with a joke.[61]

Nevertheless you felt a void in your life at that time, and—so it seemed to me—you implied that a visit from me would be welcome. It didn't take you long to put God in your mother's place. He appeared to be the only thing left to you after her departure, a new mother. First Monica was with you in place of God, and now you seem to have God with you in her place. To begin with, it was she who came between you and me; later it was the God of the Nazarene who held that place.

I have asked myself many times whether in reality it was your own mother who stole

---

[61] *Ridendo dicere verum,* from Horace's satires.

from you the will to love a woman. Wasn't it because you loved me that from the start Monica was reluctant to live in the same house as you and eat at the same table? Book III, Aurel. Wasn't that also the reason she went running to Milano wanting to get you married? Book VI! And wasn't it for that same reason that you chose Abstinence when nothing came of the arranged marriage after all?

After we had crossed the Arno River you stopped me with an affectionate hand on my shoulder and asked if you could smell my hair. "Life is so short,"[62] you said. Why did you say that, Aurel? And why did you want to smell my hair? What was it you wanted to confirm?

[62] *Vita brevis.*

It is not until the beginning of Book IV that you mention me. You write: "In those years I had a woman and lived with her, but not in what is called lawful marriage. She fell prey to my unstable and ill-considered passion. But I did have only the one, and I was faithful to her as to a spouse."[63]

When I read this section on your unstable and ill-considered passion, I had to laugh aloud, for I felt your passion was both stable and considered, I really did. Moreover, it was constant, although it could burn less brightly

[63] The quotation continues thus in *Conf.* IV, 2: "In cohabiting with her I was certainly able to learn from experience the difference between a marriage grounded on the idea of having children and a love relationship engaged in purely to satisfy one's own passion, so that the children born of it are not wished for, even though one is obliged to love them once they have arrived." Clearly, Floria is so unimpressed by this passage that she does not even trouble to comment on it. She emphasizes the opposite, namely that they lived together as spouses.

at some times than at others. Besides, I was certainly no prey. As you yourself intimate, we lived like a married couple—with the one vital difference that we had declared ourselves to each other without interference from parents. If you hadn't loved me, you would undoubtedly have taken other women, or gone to a brothel for that matter. We were not married; everyone would have understood if you had chosen another concubine in my place. But the only thing that stood between us was Monica—and, gradually, your nagging conscience telling you that perhaps you were cultivating our love so fervently that it might stand in the way of your soul's salvation.

Now you write about Claudius,[64] who died of fever. "I was miserable, and miserable is

---

[64] Augustine does not give the friend's name.

every soul bound by love to that which perishes . . . I was dreadfully weary of life and
at the same time fearful of death."[65] Then
you write: "I carried a shattered and bleeding
soul which found it unbearable to dwell in
me; but I could find nowhere to give it rest.
It did not find peace in pleasant groves, nor
in games and song, nor in scented flower gar-
dens, nor in glittering feasts, nor in the en-
joyment of sensual love, not even in books
and poetry."[66]

I well remember that time, for it was not
easy for any of us. And yet: we had each
other, and now that your friend was dead I
was your only consolation. I believe it was
then that you began searching in earnest for

[65] *Conf.* IV, 6.

[66] *Conf.* IV, 7.

a truth that could save your soul from that which perishes. I said: Hold me close. Life is so short, and we cannot be sure that there is any eternity for our frail souls. Perhaps this is our only life. You would never believe such a thing, Aurel. You would rack your brains until you found an eternity for your soul. It seemed more important to you to save it from perdition than it was to save our relationship.

So we left Tagaste and returned to Carthage. I rejoiced, for sharing a house with Monica was no life for us. You write: "Days came, and days passed, and each day that passed gave me fresh hope and new ideas, and so, little by little, I became myself again with the aid of the same joys as before."[67]

67 *Conf.* IV, 8.

But the seed was sown; a new gravity had taken possession of you.

It is strange that you do not write more about Adeodatus. Although perhaps you include him when you mention "the same joys as before"?

V

In Book V you describe the journey from Carthage to Roma. "My mother was terribly upset about my leaving and followed me out to the coast. She strove forcibly to hold me back, trying to persuade me either to go home with her or to take her along."[68] But we tricked her, Aurel. You took her to that chapel of Cyprian's where she spent the

[68] *Conf.* V, 8.

night. Then we set sail in the pitch darkness, you and I and little Adeodatus, who was now a boy of eleven. I remember you joked and said that the Queen of Carthage was going to Roma with Aeneas. And when we sailed away from Carthage, I really felt like a resurrected Dido. I thought of that strange question you had put to me more than ten years earlier: Have you been to Roma? I was so sure that what we were doing was right. If the two of us were to have a future, we would somehow have to free ourselves from Monica together.

Then, after we reached Roma, you fell into a fever, but I nursed you and prayed for you. I remember how frightened you were of dying. Again and again you asked: "Am I lost now?" For you had not yet found any salvation for your soul. You write: "The fever rose, and I was about to die and be lost. Indeed, where would I have gone if I had passed away then? Yes, to the fire and the torments that my deeds deserved according to your rightful ordinance."[69]

But by Hades, Aurel! Whatever is this but distorted mythology? You who have so fiercely ridiculed the stories of the old gods, yet you still go on believing in a God of Wrath who will punish and torment people for their deeds throughout all eternity? It was lucky you did not believe in him when you lay ill in that little room in Roma. You were just so terribly frightened of your soul

[69] *Conf.* V, 9.

going to perdition.[70] It was I who had to try to soothe your fear with some words of comfort from the philosophy of the Stoics.[71] We also spoke of the Nazarene and the Christian hope. But neither of us came near to believing in this teaching of the fire and eternal torment. We were too sophisticated for that. But is that what an esteemed imperial rhetorician thinks today? That in a few years the Bishop of Hippo Regius will be safe and

---

[70] The perdition of the soul must not be confused with the Christian concept of the judgment of God. It was a widespread view within various philosophical movements throughout the whole of antiquity that some souls were damned while others could make themselves deserving of eternal life.

[71] Stoicism was a philosophical movement that stressed spiritual equilibrium in harmony with the controlling intelligence of the world. The Stoics emphasized that all natural processes—such as disease and death—follow the inviolable laws of nature. The human being must therefore learn to resign himself to his fate.

sound in God's blissful paradise, while Floria Aemilia will be banished to eternal fire and torment because she hasn't yet consented to be baptized? No, Your Grace, you will have to adjust that teaching very quickly. If you don't, I am not a little worried that still more people will be baptized and that the universal church will grow. We are both aware of the political decadence our society has undergone recently. Then it's probably not to be wondered at that customs and beliefs undergo a similar decadence!

You soon recovered. I haven't forgotten how suddenly the fever lost its grip; in a short time you were on your feet again. Then we went into town together, you and I. For several months you taught rhetoric, at the same time finding nourishment in all the conversations with those philosophers who are called academics.[72] I was constantly allowed to accompany you, especially when you were going to meet new people. You were proud, proud as a victor to have me at your side, not so much because you had chosen me as because I had chosen you.

Not long after, you were appointed to an imperial post as tutor of rhetoric in Milano. The journey there was a great experience, and that might well have been when we two had our richest hours together. Do you remember when we set out along the Via Cassia that fine fall day—Adeodatus, you and I, and a couple of friends, Aurel, and many

[72] I.e., the Skeptics. Augustine himself describes them in these words: "They thought one should doubt everything, and declared that man cannot comprehend any truth" (*Conf.* V, 10).

we had not known before. We were a large company.

Then we arrived at the old garrison town of Florentia[73] on the Arno River. Do you remember how we stood there pointing up at the snow-covered mountains that were suddenly revealed through the trees? You only remember ideas, Aurel—can't you try to recall some real sense experiences, too? Soon we crossed the river, and while we were still on the bridge you came up behind me. You had been conversing with some men, but suddenly you were at my side. I felt your hand on my shoulder. Then you pulled me gently toward you and whispered: "Life is so short, Floria!"

[73] Florence.

You seized my wrist and held it tightly—
as if you had decided that this moment was
one you would never forget. It was then you
asked if you could smell my hair. You did so.
I felt your breath on my neck while you un-
twisted my long hair and breathed in its
scent. It was as if you wanted to draw the
whole of me into yourself, as if I had my
home within you. You seemed to want to say
that I would always belong with you because
our souls had fused together. This was before
Monica came to Milano, before those tire-
some plans for marriage, before you met the
theologians.

Now, do not come and say that what
happened on the bridge over the Arno was
merely the result of sensual passion or self-
indulgence, Good Bishop. Many people were

looking at us that day, and perhaps that very fact makes me remember it so well. There on the bridge you suddenly did something you knew I set great store by. It was a gesture to me, an expression of your deep acknowledgment of me as the woman in your life, even though I was not your wife according to law. I also think it may have been an expression of release, because at last we were able to move freely in a land far away from Monica. Were we not both in some way fugitives?

The years have gone by and much has happened since we two lived together in Italia, but the fact that you pleased me and found pleasure in the scent of my hair, now that we were on our way out into the province together, would that cause your God to damn you? Was it to redeem such sins that he let his only son be nailed to the cross? We too had a son with us on that journey—he hopped and danced around his father and mother. But nailed to a cross for the sake of love? I hope for your soul's salvation that your God has as well-developed a sense of humor as you had before you met the theologians. Even so, his must be more macabre than yours, otherwise he may come to think that your soul has deteriorated so much since you walked over the Arno River with me that it can no longer be saved. Where there is the most intellect, Your Grace, there is, as a rule, the least love![74]

[74] Probably a paraphrase of the adage *Ubi mens plurima, ibi minima fortuna* (Where there is the most intellect there is the least money).

On the other side of the bridge we passed some vendors, and I stopped to look at a beautiful cameo.[75] You bought it for me on the spot, and now I sit with it in my hand, clasping it tightly. So God will have to forgive me for holding on to the material. But it is all I have. I haven't seen a radiant vision with my inner eye, nor have I discovered anything supernatural or heard voices. In that way I am still a simple woman. I wish you nothing but the best for the salvation of your soul.[76] But life is short and I know so little. What if there is no heaven above us,

[75] A precious stone, shell, or other material carved in relief. A particularly popular art form in this period.

[76] *Nil nisi bene.* Here she may be playing on the saying *De mortuis nil nisi bene* (Nothing but good of the dead). If so, it must be interpreted as an insinuation that Aurel's soul is no longer living.

Aurel? Imagine that this life is what we were created for! Then, may our souls soar above the Arno for all eternity. For was it not in Florentia that Floria flourished,[77] and was it not in the evening sunshine over the Arno that Aurel's brow gleamed gold?[78]

[77] *In Florentia Floria floruit.*

[78] *Auro,* "like gold." Some of the wordplay is lost in translation.

VI

Then, finally, you met Bishop Ambrosius in Milano. You write that you thought him a fortunate man "in the eyes of the world because he was held in high esteem by powerful men."[79] Only his unmarried state troubled you. Oh, such spiritual agony you had to go through for allowing yourself to be convinced that you would have to reject love itself for the sake of your soul's salvation!

[79] *Conf.* VI, 3.

Monica arrived in late spring. She had followed you over land and sea, you say. She put herself between us, with her back to me, although she knew we were one. She had two aims: one was to have you baptized, the other to get you married to a girl of high rank. I think the latter was the most important. You yourself were in doubt about everything, but you decided "for the time being to become a catechumen in the Catholic church, as my parents had advised me, until a light should appear by which I could confidently direct my course."[80] In Book VI you exclaim: "Oh, academics, you who are such great men! Can we find no certainty to build our life on?"[81]

[80] *Conf.* V, 14.

[81] *Conf.* VI, 11. Cf. footnote 72.

Now you must forgive me for copying out a rather long passage, but you show here a few sporadic attempts to collect your wits. You write: "What if death puts an end to all agony of soul at the moment it severs consciousness? Indeed, *that* is a question for discussion. But it cannot be so. Far from it! It is not without reason that the Christian faith spreads and is so highly regarded throughout the world. God would never have done such great and remarkable things for us if the death of the body were the end of the soul's life as well. Why do we still hesitate to relinquish all worldly hope and to devote ourselves solely to seeking God and true happiness in life? But wait! After all, there are joys in this world as well, and they have their own charm, which is no small thing.

We should not be too quick to put an end to our inclinations in that direction. For it would be somewhat unseemly to return to these pleasures later. Is it not a great achievement to attain high position? What more can one wish for? I have plenty of influential friends. If nothing else, I could get an appointment—so as not to set my sights on something higher too quickly. Then I can take a wife with a substantial fortune, so she would not impose a heavier financial burden on me. That should be a suitable goal. Many great men worthy of being considered exemplars have devoted themselves to the study of wisdom even though they married. That was how I used to talk, and my heart was blown hither and thither by changing winds. Meanwhile time passed, and I delayed turning to the Lord. From day to day I postponed living in you, but I did not put off death from affecting me daily."[82]

Life, that is, although here you call it death, and it is you who do this, you who once bent over to smell my hair when we were crossing the Arno River together. You go on: "I loved life's true happiness, but feared to seek it where it is to be found. And at the same time as I sought it, I fled from it. For I thought I would be far too unhappy if I had to go without a woman's embrace."[83]

It was *my* embrace you could not do without, Aurel. That was something we two

[82] *Conf.* VI, 11.

[83] Ibid.

talked of many times. Couldn't you write it? Ah, well, one must be cautious about naming names.[84]

You also discussed such things constantly with Alypius:[85] "Neither of us was especially attracted to what makes marriage something beautiful, the task of creating a good home and bringing up children. The chief concern was that I was accustomed to satisfying my insatiable sexual desire, which kept me captive and plagued me violently."[86]

---

[84] *Nomina sunt odiosa*, i.e., "names are objectionable," presumably taken from Cicero's speech to Roscius.

[85] Friend and earlier pupil of Augustine, from his birthplace, Tagaste. Alypius went to Rome before Augustine did to study law. Then they journeyed together to Milan (*Conf.* VI, 7–10).

[86] *Conf.* VI, 12.

What in reality plagued you was that marriage—for which I was unfit merely owing to my lack of worldly goods—would entail your betrayal of me. For were we not twin souls, Aurel? Hadn't we grown so close in both body and soul that to divide us would be better left to a surgeon than to a mother playing the part of suitor? And didn't we also have Adeodatus to think of, who was twelve by then?[87]

---

[87] Augustine must have gone through great agonies of soul when he deserted his lover, even though this is not touched upon in the *Confessions*. There he does not give so much as a thought to the wounds he inflicted on Floria. But even in his text *De bono coniugali* (*On the Benefits of Marriage*, 401), written at the time he could have received Floria's letter, Augustine points out that a man who dismisses a faithful lover in order to marry another woman is guilty of infidelity. Not all Christians shared this view. It was generally accepted until well into the Middle Ages that a man could have a concubine before he married. For example, Bishop Leo of Rome in the middle of the fifth century said it was

You write: "I was strongly advised to get married. I proposed and was accepted. My mother was enthusiastically absorbed in this. She wanted me first to get married and then be cleansed in the saving waters of baptism."[88]

---

permissible for a Christian man to leave a concubine in order to marry. This was regarded not as divorce or bigamy but, on the contrary, as moral improvement. Augustine at the time rejected such an idea, believing that a man who has entered a relationship with a cohabitee should stay with his partner and not go off to marry another woman.

I think it is interesting to ask whether Augustine—so soon after writing the *Confessions*—would have adopted this view, which in fact defend the "married" status or rights of the concubine, if he had not read the letter from Floria. So in the end perhaps she really was right in saying that her letter to Aurel was a letter to the whole Christian church.

As recently as 1930 Pius XI quoted from Augustine's text *On the Benefits of Marriage*. Without realizing it, he may in a way have been influenced by Floria's letter. However, I have my own reasons for believing that both he and popes before him have been conversant with the *Codex Floriae*.

[88] *Conf.* VI, 13.

At that point, Monica sought me out. I can't forget the morning she suddenly appeared in the room as I was washing. You had just left for the school of rhetoric and would be there all day. I was told to pack up and make myself scarce. Everything was arranged for the whole journey to Africa: a company was leaving that same afternoon. You had proposed to a girl and been accepted. But the girl's parents had demanded that I be removed from your side as quickly as possible.

I thought that this was Monica's revenge for what had happened when we left her in Carthage that night. It seemed that now we would both learn who was the stronger. She said it was up to her to get me out of the way because you couldn't bring yourself to do it. Like the peasant who can't bring himself to slaughter his own lamb. And I believed her, that was my tragic flaw![89] For it must have struck you that I was just such a tragic figure of a woman—as if drawn out of Euripides' toga.[90] I was betrayed by my own spouse for the sake of heavenly love! That is how it was, Aurel, that is exactly how it was![91]

I believed it was your premeditated wish that I return to Carthage, where we had once

[89] *Peccatum*, fault or offense. Cf. Greek *hamartia*, the term for the flaw that eventually leads to the fall of the tragic hero. This fatal step is generally made with the best of intentions, and it is this condition that makes it tragic.

[90] The Greeks used *himation*, not *toga*, the Latin name for the Roman national costume. However, Floria uses the word *toga*.

[91] *Sic, Aureli! Sic!*

sat together under a fig tree. Not until we met again in Roma were you able to swear that I was sent away from you without your knowledge or will.

In her role as intermediary Monica also said you bade me promise not to live with any other man. I interpreted this as a sign that you had not yet really decided to marry, and that perhaps we might come to hold each other again. To this day it has been a mystery to me why Monica should say such a thing, for I was quite sure that all she had in mind was to get rid of me. Was it merely to make my leaving smoother? Or perhaps she thought it would be easier for me to accept baptism if I didn't find another man to live with. But then I soon received the letter from you, in which you fervently begged me not to give myself to anyone else. You even wrote that probably nothing would come of the marriage. But most important of all, you ended the letter from Milano with these words: "I miss you, Floria. Floria, I miss you!"

You had taken Adeodatus with you to the school of rhetoric that day; I wasn't even able to kiss him one last time before I had to pack up my possessions and part from man and child. In this way I took everything away with me.[92]

I didn't do what Dido did, Aurel, so perhaps I promised too much that day beneath

[92] Must be a play on Cicero, who ascribes the statement *Omnia mea mecum porto* to the Greek philosopher Bias, who was obliged to flee his enemy without taking anything with him. But, in fact, he did take everything he possessed: it was only his wisdom and experience that were of any real value.

the fig tree. If I had had Adeodatus with me, I would not have done what Medea did either.[93] But I did go away.

---

[93] From Euripides' tragedy of Medea, who killed her own children because her husband, Jason, deceived her. Thus, Medea's hatred of Jason was stronger than her love for the children they had together. In their devastating passion Dido and Medea resemble each other not a little.

VII

You write about how eagerly Monica worked to have you married: "The girl I had proposed to was about two years under marriageable age. But since I liked her, I was willing to wait."[94] Well, I think you should have written that you liked waiting!

I myself find it rather disappointing that

[94] *Conf.* VI, 13. The usual marriageable age was twelve to thirteen years. We can thus assume—as Floria writes earlier—that the girl was only eleven.

you don't append so much as a sentence on what you thought about your mother's taking matters into her own hands and sending me away while you were out with Adeodatus. You went home to an empty house. And I—with whom you had traveled all the way from Africa—had vanished. I, Aurel, with whom you had walked across the Arno River, wasn't there anymore. You merely write: "The woman I lived with was not permitted to stay at my side. They took her away from me because she stood in the way of my marriage. My heart, which was deeply attached to her, was pierced, and wounded so that it bled. She returned to Africa and promised you she would never live with any other man. She left our natural son with me. But I, unhappy man, could not follow her example. When I thought that it would be two years before I could have the girl I had proposed to, I did not have the patience to wait. For though my opinion of marriage was not high, I was a slave to my lust. Therefore I took another woman, but not as a wife. Thus my soul's sickness remained unchanged. Indeed, it grew even worse as I waited for marriage, supported by old habit."[95]

I had not heard a word about this other woman before reading your confessions. How ashamed you must have been, for I was not going to give myself to another man. Still, it is useful to know about this, for here you admit that it was really not because you were to be married that I was sent away.

[95] *Conf.* VI, 15.

Wouldn't it have been better for us to have each other during the time you waited for the unfortunate child to reach marriageable age? You never wanted marriage; you wanted to save your soul from eternal annihilation. But then you had a perfectly ordinary relapse into "sensual lust," and such things can happen. Poor you, Aurel, I begin to understand your profound need to make some sort of confession of sins. I am merely a little disappointed with your selection.

I assume Monica did not frown on your new prey. She had managed to wipe out the years-long relationship with the woman you loved heart and soul. So the next woman, by merely satisfying bodily desire, was probably a good substitute. Your mother was a tolerant woman, Your Grace, and nothing but

good must be said of the dead. In the end,
she took her cruel revenge for what had
happened that night we two set sail from
Africa.

You write: "My wound, inflicted when my
relationship with the woman I lived with
was brought to an end, would not heal either.
At first it was inflamed and agonizing, but
then it festered, and I became less sensitive
to the pain. But my situation grew more and
more hopeless."[96] And you go on: "The only
thing that kept me back from an even deeper
maelstrom of sensual passions was the fear
of death and your coming judgment, which
never left me, however much I changed my
views . . . In my heart I would have given

---

[96] Ibid.

Epicurus the prize[97] if I had not believed there was any life for the soul after death or any retribution for what we have done. But Epicurus would not believe that. I asked: If we were immortal and could live in eternal sensual pleasure without fear of losing it, why should we not be happy? And why should we seek anything else?"[98]

No, why should we seek anything else? I mean: Why should we search for something

---

[97] Epicurus (341–270 B.C.), Greek philosopher, resident of Athens. Epicurus concurred with Democritus' atomism and believed materialistic philosophy could relieve the human fear of death and the punishment of the gods. "Death does not concern us," he said. "For as long as we live, death is not here. And when death comes, we are no longer alive." He summed up his liberating philosophy with what he called the "four healing herbs": "The gods are not to be feared. Death is nothing to worry about. The good is easy to attain. The frightful is easy to bear."

[98] *Conf.* VI, 16.

that may not exist? You remind me a little of that Greek who won some gold coins in a game, then wanted more and gambled away his whole fortune.[99]

Picture a luxuriant scene with people and animals, flowers and children, wine and honey. In this landscape there is also a frightful labyrinth. Now imagine, Pious Bishop, you who were once my playfully teasing little bedfellow, imagine you have gotten lost inside this labyrinth. You can't find an Ariadne's thread[100] to lead you out of the maze

[99] I have been unable to discover which Greek Floria refers to.

[100] Ariadne gave Theseus a ball of twine when he was about to enter the labyrinth on Crete (Knossos) to kill the monster Minotaur, which demanded seven young women and seven young men from Athens every ninth year. With the aid of the twine, Theseus was able to find his way out.

of paths and back to the paradise you were living in. All the theologians and Platonists reign deep within the labyrinth, and each man who enters increases their number. For every one of them is misled into believing that everything outside the labyrinth is the devil's work. Now it is your turn to be misled, and soon you stop wanting to get out. That is because you, too, have joined the theologians' band; you, too, have become one of those devourers of men in the depths of the dark labyrinth.[101] Or perhaps I should say, rather, a fisher of men?[102] You don't forget the woman you loved, but you praise God

[101] Cf. previous footnote.

[102] *Piscator hominum.* In the Vulgate, Mark 1:17 reads: *Et dixit eis Iesus venite post me et faciam vos fieri piscatores hominum.* Cf. Matthew 4:19.

that you are now separated from her. For now she can no longer tempt you. Only in your dreams do "images of things that were fixed by old habit live on."[103]

May God forgive you. Perhaps he is somewhere watching you scorn all his works. So many times in your confessions you say that in your earlier life you were where God is not. But suppose that only now you are on the wrong road? Oedipus also believed he was on the right road when he traveled from Delphi to Thebes. That was *his* tragic mistake. Everything would have been much better if he had gone home to his foster parents in Corinth instead. Much better, Aurel, if

[103] *Conf.* X, 30. I wonder whether Floria's simile was written as a conscious attempt to formulate a contrast with Plato's cave simile, which she would most probably have known.

you had found your way back to Carthage. Here we can still glimpse God's love in flowers and trees—and in Venus, Aurel.

I would remind you of some words from Horace: "Always believe that each day that dawns is your last."[104] Of course it isn't certain that this is your last day, but it may well turn out to be. In this light, perhaps there is no life for our souls after this one. It could be so, old rhetorician, and now I want you to consider such a possibility once again. To think that the Bishop of Hippo may have made an error!

Life is short, all too short. But perhaps it is here and now that we live, and only here and now. If so, haven't you turned your back

[104] *Omnem crede diem tibi diluxisse supremum.*

on those days that in spite of everything shine—and lost your way in a dark and gloomy labyrinth of ideas where I cannot reach you and lead you out again?

We don't live forever, Aurel. That does not mean that we shouldn't seize the days we are given.

About your soul—which you love above everything—you write toward the end of Book VII: "Wherever it turned, on its back, on its side, or on its stomach, everywhere was *hard*. In you alone is rest."[105]

I'm led to think again of all the days and nights we spent together in Carthage. We found a deep rest in each other as well. It was then you said: "Where you are, I want to be."

[105] *Conf.* VI, 16; "with you," i.e., with God.

But you didn't keep that promise. Like a thief you stole away from me and crept into the maze of theology without taking my guiding thread with you.[106]

You start Book VII with these words: "By now my wicked and sinful youth was at an end, and I embarked on the years of manhood. But the older I became, the more reason I had to be ashamed of my emptiness."[107] Although what is sin, Your Grace? And what is wickedness? Or emptiness? Isn't it everything that keeps us from God?

You continue: "I could imagine no other reality than that which we normally see with our two eyes."[108] But now imagine

[106] See footnote 100.

[107] *Conf.* VII, 1.

[108] Ibid.

there is no other reality! If that's the case, you have turned not toward the light but away from it!

Can't you see the trees for the leaves, Aurel?[109] Can you still see that there is a world around you? If what you see with the naked eye doesn't please you, you can always blind yourself. Although to me that would be the same as blasphemy.

You write further that gradually you understood clearly and knew with certainty that "what is perishable is inferior to what is imperishable."[110] This sounds acceptably wise and considered, I admit. Although the question is whether, taking everything into

---

[109] *Frondem in silvis non cernis?* Roughly approximates: "Can't you see the forest for the trees?"

[110] *Conf.* VII, 1.

account, there *is* such a thing as "the imperishable" for our souls to cling to. And if there isn't anything imperishable to catch hold of, then in my opinion it is sillier to search for the imperishable than to seek the perishable. Now, I assume that your eyes have not yet been gouged out and, for that matter, that the Bishop of Hippo hasn't castrated himself for the sake of the kingdom of heaven. Poetic enthusiasm, Aurel. Can you forgive me?

You go on in this vein to record what you have seen with your inner eye and to express your love for that which has no body. I shudder. Imagine finding someone who had the power of silencing birdsong merely because he had heard a still more beautiful song with his inner ear? Or imagine someone with the power of making every flower and tree

wither because he had smelled a better per-
fume than nature's own scents with his inner nose? Indeed, imagine someone who had
the power to smash every house and every
object of art in the whole world because
he had invested all his love in immaterial
things?

For me the birds ceased to sing. The flowers were not as colorful as before. No one
smelled my hair. And no one embraced me.
So I did share some of Dido's fate after all.
But I shall not let go of the cameo I hold in
my hand.

VIII

In Book VIII you describe your own conversion in Milano, for, after all, you did find a kind of peace. You write: "By then I was convinced of eternal life in you, even if I only saw it through a glass darkly.[111] But I had been released from all doubts about the ex-

---

[111] See 1 Corinthians 13:12. In the Vulgate: *Videmus nunc per speculum in enigmate, tunc autem facie ad faciem, nunc cognosco ex parte, tunc autem cognoscam sicut et cognitus sum* (For now we see through a glass, darkly; but then face to face: now I know in part; but then shall I know even as also I am known).

istence of an imperishable being from whom all other beings originate."[112]

All right, dear Aurel, it may be that an imperishable being who has created the whole world and all other living creatures on earth, women and children included, does exist. What remains a puzzle to me are the conclusions you draw from your belief.

"I was displeased with myself for leading a worldly life," you write. "It was like a heavy burden weighing me down."[113] And you elaborate on what you mean by a worldly life: "I was still firmly bound to the love of a woman. The apostle did not forbid me to marry; but he exhorted me to some-

[112] *Conf.* VIII, 1.

[113] Ibid.

thing better, saying he would far prefer all men to emulate him. But weak as I was, I chose the path of least resistance. That alone was to blame for my lurching listlessly in other ways as well. I grew ill, preyed upon by consuming worries."[114]

A little later you add: "Thus within me were two conflicting wills, one old and the other new, one carnal and the other spiritual. And through this strife they caused a split in my mind."[115]

It must have been at this time that you wrote me a letter, where you also speak about how sorely you miss our embraces. But you must not let this letter worry you, I shall not show it to the priest.

[114] Ibid.

[115] *Conf.* VIII, 5.

Your confessions continue: "Thus I was pleasantly held down by the burden of this world, rather as when one is asleep. And the thoughts of you I was struggling with resembled the efforts people make when they are trying to wake up but are overwhelmed by fatigue and sink back into deep sleep. Naturally, no one wants to be asleep constantly. Any sane person thinks it best to be awake. All the same, when our limbs are heavy and relaxed, we often delay shaking off slumber and prefer to stay asleep, even though we don't really enjoy it and it's time to get up. Likewise, I was sure it was better to give myself over to your love than to give in to my passions."[116]

Really, Aurel! Are you going to say it yet

[116] Ibid.

again? I think you're repeating yourself now, not so untypically in fact. You always could harp on the same thing! And now you just go on and on again: "Many years of my life had passed—about twelve—since at the age of nineteen I had read Cicero's *Hortensius* and the desire for wisdom awakened in me. But I put off despising earthly happiness and devoting myself to the search for this true happiness. Not merely finding it but the very seeking of it is preferable to having known all the world's treasures and kingdoms and physical joys, even though they might be floating around at one's disposal."[117]

You go on about how God released you

[117] *Conf.* VIII, 7.

from the chains of sensual lust. "Give me purity and abstinence, but not yet!" you prayed. "For I was afraid you would grant my prayers at once, and heal me of the disease of sensual lust immediately. But I preferred to have it satisfied rather than to end it . . . I was not totally willing, yet not totally unwilling."[118]

Eventually your new bride came and embraced you, "fair and cheerful, but not frivolous in her joy."[119]

I am almost moved to congratulate you, for in one way you did in fact get married, to an invisible queen it is true, but she was, after all, the one you desired. In that way, too,

[118] *Conf.* VIII, 7 and 10.

[119] *Conf.* VIII, 11.

you could marry without being obliged to bring some new woman into your mother's house. So Monica gained the upper hand. She must have been greatly pleased—you don't try to hide that. She had you both married and baptized at the same time.

You write of having violent emotions after your conversion—I was about to say wedding: "Then a great storm broke out, bringing with it a huge flood of tears. To allow them to flow freely, I rose and walked away from Alypius. If I was going to weep, I felt it more suitable to be alone. I went far enough away so as not to be embarrassed by his presence. That was how I felt then, and he realized it. I think I said something or other that caused my voice to reveal I was on the point of weeping. And so I rose. Alypius stayed where he was, in great amazement. Without being aware of it, I threw myself down beneath a fig tree and let the tears run freely. They streamed from my eyes like a pleasing sacrifice to you."[120]

So you sought shelter again beneath a fig tree; and, in a way, that closed the circle, for you must have thought of our fig tree here at home in Carthage. "Have you been to Roma?" you had asked. A chill runs down my back when I think of that, for in the light of your confessions, what happened at that time becomes almost prophetic. Can it be that any of those tears streaming from your eyes were for me as well?

Not until you collapsed under a fig tree in

[120] *Conf.* VIII, 12.

Milano had Aeneas found his promised land.
Now it was perfected: everything had con-
quered love![121]

You write: "Then we go to my mother. We
tell her what has happened. Oh, how she re-
joices! . . . For you had converted me to yourself so that now I wished for neither a wife
nor anything else on which we put our faith
in this world. I stood on that tree trunk of
faith where you had brought my mother to
see me in a vision many years earlier. You
turned her sorrow to joy, a joy far richer
than what she had wished for, and much
more precious and purer than what she had

---

[121] *Omnia vicerant amorem.* I imagine Floria has turned Virgil's
"love conquers all" on its head here. For in Virgil as well the word
order is *omnia vincit amor.* Aeneas, incidentally, was the son of
Aphrodite (Venus), the goddess of love.

once expected to get by having a grandchild through me."[122]

All the same, weren't you too quick to write off Adeodatus' potential in this sphere? At that point you could not know anything about his unhappy fate. Or did the poor boy allow himself to be embraced by Abstinence as well? Or perhaps you no longer considered him your son? Oh, well, he was a bastard, of course, and we have not yet reached the last act of the tragedy.

About the return journey to Verecundus from the country estate you write in Book IX: "We took with us Adeodatus, my natural son, the fruit of my sin. You had endowed him well. He was about fifteen years

---

[122] *Conf.* VIII, 12.

old, but his intelligence surpassed that of many worthy and learned men. I praise you for your gifts, Lord my God, you who created all things and have the power to make something beautiful out of our vileness. For I had no other part in that boy than the sin. And the discipline we raised him with from early childhood was due solely to your encouragement. I praise you for your gifts."[123]

You go on: "There is a book I wrote entitled *The Teacher*. It is a conversation between him and me. You know that all thoughts expressed through the mouth of the person conversing with me are real ideas Adeodatus had in his sixteenth year. I heard many other things from him that were more remarkable. I trembled with awe at his in-

[123] *Conf.* IX, 6.

telligence. And who else but you can perform such marvels? You took him early from this life here on earth. So I can think of him all the more confidently without anxiety for his childhood or youth or the whole of his life."[124]

I make no secret of the intense pain it causes me to read these lines. I tremble, too, but for another reason. I don't know whether it was God who took Adeodatus away from life here on earth. I have no opinion on that. I know only that it was you who took him away from his mother. Adeodatus was my only child, Your Grace! Was it not in your care that he finally faded away and died, leaving us both?

How happy you must now be not having

[124] *Conf.* IX, 6.

to worry about Adeodatus being lured beneath a fig tree by a capricious woman. I myself would have been more worried about him one day falling to his knees before Abstinence—as her slave and henpecked husband.[125]

[125] Here Floria uses the word *crepundia*, which should probably be translated as "rattle" (a child's toy), "bangles," or "baubles," from *crepo*, "rattle," "jangle," or "clatter." But cf. also *crepida*, Greek "sandal," a derivative of the same verb! Directly translated, then, Floria describes Aurel as Abstinence's "bauble."

IX

Following your style, I'm leaving out a great deal to get to what is essential more quickly. Besides, I have spent half my fortune on parchment and don't have many sheets left to write on.

On your way back to Africa you arrived at Ostia on the Tiber. There you and Monica had a "wonderful conversation" in which you sought "to discover the nature of the eternal life in which the saints shall participate." The conversation led you to "conclude that the greatest pleasure the bodily senses can give, in the most radiant earthly glory, is, next to the joy of eternity, not even worthy of comparison, let alone mention."[126]

You must forgive me, Your Grace, but I am a cultivated woman now. So in all humility I feel a certain need to suggest that this sounds like some kind of conjuration. For what if you should be wrong on precisely this decisive point? At one time you would have given the prize to Epicurus—so you said when we were still together. I myself believe that you and Adeodatus would have come back to Carthage at once. For then you would have had no choice, then you would

126 *Conf.* IX, 10.

have had to live as a whole human being here and now, and I think you would have had more than enough earthly love to share with both me and others.

Life is so short, we do not have time to pronounce any damning judgment on love. We must first live, Aurel, then we can philosophize.

But we must on no account forget Monica. For it was in Ostia that she fell ill with a fever. And you learned that "with motherly confidence" she had talked to some of your friends "about despising this life, and about how good it is to die."[127] *Sic!*

She was a pious person—I mean, one who managed to despise this life. However, I feel

[127] *Conf.* IX, 11.

compelled to add that this might be tantamount to despising God's work of creation. For we do not know if God has created any other world for us. I realize I am starting to repeat myself, but that may well be because you repeat yourself just as much in your confessions, Your Grace. I am of the opinion that it must be human arrogance to reject this life—with all its earthly joys—in favor of an existence which is, perhaps, merely an abstraction. Surely you haven't forgotten Aristotle's criticism of all such notions of an ideal world?

Life is so short, Aurel. We are free to hope for a life after this one. But we are not free to treat each other or ourselves badly, almost like an instrument with which to attain an existence we know nothing about. Besides, there is something else to which you give absolutely no consideration in any of your books. As imperial rhetorician, you should at least have discussed the possibility of there being an eternal life for individual souls, but the grounds for judgment are different from those you yourself almost take for granted. For instance, I believe it is not necessarily a greater sin to engage in physical love with the woman in one's life than it is to separate that same woman from her only son. I myself take pleasure in the idea that the God who created heaven and earth is the same God who created Venus. Do you remember when I was with child? Or when I nurtured little Adeodatus at my breast? Even then you dared to hold me, and you sought no other.

Was that the time when you were furthest away from God?

I'm not saying I know any of this. I'm only

saying I don't know. I'm not even saying that I don't believe in God's judgment. I'm only saying that I may also believe in the judgment against turning one's back on all the joys, all the warmth, and all the tenderness that the Bishop of Hippo Regius now denies. This is Floria's confession!

Then Monica died on the ninth day of her illness, in her fifty-sixth year, and in my thirty-third, Aurel. "This devout and pious soul was released from the body."[128] You write: "When she had drawn her last breath, my boy, Adeodatus, began to weep loudly with sorrow." But you "felt it was not seemly to grieve for the dead with tears and moans. For that may be suitable where the

[128] Ibid.

dead are mourned because of their miserable lot or because their death is seen as complete annihilation. But death was no misfortune for Mother. In fact, it was no death."[129]

Peace be to her memory, Bishop! You do not conceal the fact that you too felt pain, bitter pain, and as soon as you were alone you allowed the tears to flow freely. It is true that you are slightly ashamed of weeping over your mother, for that could be seen as a sign that you still nourished earthly feelings.

Do you remember we once talked of the arrogance of the Greek heroes?[130] I think it

[129] *Conf.* IX, 12.

[130] Cf. the Greek word *hybris*—which was met with the gods' wrath (*nemesis*). Floria uses the Latin word *superbia* here.

isn't out of place here to remind you that you, too, are merely human.[131] For how long, Aurel, will you try my patience?[132] No matter how much you squirm, you too have "earthly feelings," if you have any feelings at all. I mean, what other feelings would those you especially possess be?

Then I received the second letter from my Aurel . . .

After Monica was buried at Ostia,[133] you went to Roma with Adeodatus, and both of

[131] *Te hominem esse memento.* These words were to be whispered in the ear of a victor during his triumphal procession through Rome.

[132] Cf. Cicero in his first speech to Catiline: "How long, Catiline, will you abuse our patience?"

[133] Monica's grave in Ostia was found in the summer of 1945 in front of the church of Santa Aurea by two boys digging a hole for a basketball goalpost.

you stayed there for nearly a year. But you do not write anything about this year in your confessions, Your Grace. Why not? Is there, after all, a limit to your need to confess?

To confess is medicine for one who has gone astray, writes Cicero.[134] But you do not confess to your gravest faults! How can you just cross out the last act of the tragedy? For what can we learn from the tragedy if we delete *that*?

After Monica died you must have felt cast into a state of doubt and emptiness. For now you were left alone with a son, Monica was gone, and you missed me, Aurel, you missed me. Adeodatus must have done so as well—

[134] *Fit erranti medicina confessio.*

it was two years since he had seen me. But he was never to see me again, and I never saw him either.

You wrote in your letter that Monica was dead, and I shall not plague you by quoting everything here and now. But you were eager to tell me that the engagement had long since been annulled and that you would never marry. You might need to be reminded of your concluding greetings. You wrote: "How I miss you, Floria! I wish you could be with us now. I want to see you, I both want to see you and at the same time don't want to. I want to, but I cannot, and I cannot, but I would."

Sometimes it's hard for a person to make a decision, and is it so strange that sometimes the decision is the wrong one? "I know what is good for me, but do what is harmful to me," writes Ovid.[135]

It was then that you allowed Adeodatus to add a few words in the letter to his mother. So sweet of you, Aurel, and so thoughtful, for he must have felt such pleasure now that a couple of years had passed since he and I had last seen each other.

It was a mutual loss, and I interpreted your words to mean you wanted to see me. So I journeyed to Roma. I was lucky and obtained passage in just a few days.

One question rang in my ears the whole time: "Have you been to Roma?" When I arrived there for the second time, and this time

---

[135] *Video meliora proboque, deteriora sequor.* Cf. Romans 7:19. In the Vulgate: *Non enim quod volo bonum hoc facio sed quod nolo malum hoc ago.*

quite alone, I had to go around to the con-
gregations asking for you. But after only a
few days we met up on the Aventine, and we
were able to embrace each other once again.

We stayed a long time like that, looking
deep into each other's eyes, as deep as our
gaze could reach. Didn't it seem in that hour
that we were a single living soul that somehow reflected itself? Then you said something, Aurel, do you remember? "Now you
must be with me always," you said!

You did not *fall* when, for a few short
weeks, we resumed our old life together. I
mean, you rose up to new life after having
lived in the theologians' valley of shadows.
So what happened during those weeks in-
volves nothing for you to confess to either
God or men. I hope it is out of regard for

what happened later that you write nothing about that time in your books.

Do you remember when we were down in the Forum looking up at the snow that had fallen on the imperial palaces? You saw that I was cold, and then you drew me close, so close I could feel how your blood grew warm. I remember I turned to you and said you had no shame. But I wanted it, too. We were two people, although we had only one desire.

We couldn't live under the same roof, for you didn't want Adeodatus to meet me, at least not at first, you said. I could have died with longing to see him. But you thought he would be so disappointed if, after seeing me, something should happen to prevent our permanent reunion. So you rented this room up on the Aventine, a place where only you and I could see each other.

How can we forget that winter, Aurel? Again we were both in Venus's court with the freedom to play in her arms. Didn't you say that you felt like a withered tree that suddenly rises again because rain has fallen after a long, dry summer?

It is not merely to shield you that I keep this brief. One afternoon you turned to me in a sudden rage—it was after we had shared the gifts of Venus again. And you hit me. Do you remember how you hit me? You, Aurel, you who were once a respected teacher of rhetoric, you beat me almost senseless because you had allowed yourself to be tempted by my tenderness. So it was I who had to bear the blame for your lust. I have already cited Horace, but I will gladly do so again: When foolish people want to avoid making a mistake, they usually do the opposite thing!

You hit me and screamed, Bishop, because now I posed a threat to the salvation of your soul. Then you seized a stick and beat me again. I wondered if you might want to beat the life out of me, for that would certainly serve the same purpose as if you had castrated yourself. I was not afraid for my own skin. I was just so broken, so disappointed, and so ashamed of my Aurel that I clearly and distinctly remember wishing that you would do away with me once and for all.

Suddenly I had become something you could not just turn your back on for the sake of your soul's salvation. I myself had become

the bleeding sacrificial lamb that was necessary for the gates of heaven to open.

Then you wept—I shall not forget that.
You had stopped hitting me, but I had several
bleeding wounds. You wept, and you com-
forted me, and you begged me for forgive-
ness. Everything was so different now that
Monica was no longer here, you explained.

You folded your hands and begged, now
me, now your God, for pardon. You found
some cloth and bound my wounds. I myself
was merely cold and frightened, cold because
I was still bleeding, and frightened because I
had seen right into a kind of wickedness I
had had no inkling of.

It was as if something completely new had
begun, a new time. The old time: that ended
when we crossed the Arno River together. It

was followed by several years of great confusion and doubt. Then the new time began,
when you suddenly hit me. I had only one
thought: "You, Aurel! You!"

You sent me back to Carthage. I heard no
more from you before Adeodatus died two
years later.

X

The tragedy is ended, Bishop. There remains only the satyr play.[136] For I have also copied some extracts from Book X.

I have mentioned several times already

---

[136] In the classical period, performances of the Greek tragedies were followed by so-called satyr plays. The satyrs were lively, riotous, and half-divine beings characterized as goatlike creatures in human form. I see a weighty dose of irony in Floria's description of Augustine's Book X as a satyr play, particularly perhaps in her suggestion that a (half-divine) bishop continues to bemoan his lustful urges and needs to his dying day.

how you deal with sense after sense and passion after passion as you praise the Lord because you have hardly any earthly feelings anymore. It must be difficult for you to regulate your daily intake of food so that it is precisely enough to maintain your health but but not a fraction more. So you wage "a daily war, often in fasting" as you keep your "body in bondage." You write: "For this is not something I can decide to give up once and for all and never return to, as I was able to do with sexual intercourse."[137]

And there we are again, for it was there I wanted to go. You write: "You have forbidden relations outside marriage. And even if you allow marriage, you have encouraged us

[137] *Conf.* X, 31.

to take up something better. And because you gave me abstinence, this took place even before I became a minister of your sacrament. But in my memory, which I have spoken of so much, there still live images of acts firmly imprinted from old habit. They force themselves upon me, albeit not strongly when I am awake; but in sleep they tempt me, not only to pleasure but to assent and act upon them. These ensnaring images have such power over my soul and body that what I see in sleep persuades me to give way to actions which nothing I see when I am awake would make me succumb to. Lord, my God, I am not myself then, am I?"[138]

No, Aurel, perhaps you are only a shadow

[138] *Conf.* X, 30.

of yourself. It would probably have been better for you to be a poor slave on earth than
a high priest in the theologians' gloomy
labyrinth.[139]

Once more you will pray to your God for
help in such questions: "Is not your mercy
more than generous enough to eradicate the
impure passions that still possess me even in
sleep? Indeed, Lord, you will let your gifts of
grace increase more and more in me, so my
soul—released from the snares of lust—can
accompany me to you. Then it will no longer

[139] Presumably Floria plays on Achilles' words on the shadow life
of the kingdom of death: "I would rather be above ground still and
laboring for some poor portionless man, than be lord over all
the lifeless dead" (Homer, *The Odyssey*, trans. Walter Shewring
[World's Classics, Oxford University Press]). Thus Floria makes
Augustine one of the living dead—in the church's kingdom of
death—as he himself countless times compares a life of "sensual
passion" with death.

be at war with itself, and will not, owing to sensual images, force the body into such shameful indecency in sleep as to give vent to sinful emissions, nay, it will not even want them. You can cause it not to desire that kind of thing."[140]

Poor Aurel! He who desires much, lacks much, writes Horace.[141] For you are almost fifty already. I am tempted to say I am impressed. Besides, I feel quite proud to have had such a lasting effect on you. On that spring day in Carthage when you came and sat under the fig tree with me, I had no presentiment that our love would be so tempestuous. But "bodily passions" cannot be

[140] *Conf.* X, 30.

[141] *Multa petentibus desunt multa.*

obliterated by abstinence, this much I now realize. For the wolf only changes its skin, Your Grace, it does not change its nature![142] Or as Zeno would have put it: Why should it be so hard to run away from one's own shadow?[143]

So if we enjoy the taste of food or love, we must know how to steer away from both. You also write that you are ready to dispense with the temptations of the sense of smell forever. I have asked myself what will be left in the end, Your Grace, of our life on earth,

[142] A play on the saying *Lupus pilum mutat, non mentem.*

[143] Zeno of Elea, Greek philosopher of about 460 B.C., known for his proofs of the impossibility of diversity and movement, e.g., the paradox of Achilles and the tortoise. However, the play here is on a quotation not documented in any existing source. Most probably it is Floria's memory that is at fault here.

I mean. For hearing, too, offers its perilous enticements, you know. You write: "The joys hearing can give us had taken a firm hold on me and forced me to bow under their yoke. But you have released me and liberated me. I admit that I still find satisfaction in the melodies to which your words give life and soul when they are sung artistically by a fine voice . . . So I sin in this without noticing; but afterward I feel it is sin."[144] Sometimes you could wish that all the wonderful tunes to which the Psalms of David are sung were removed, not only from your ears but from those of the whole church, you write. And you go on: "I think, then, that Bishop Athanasius of Alexandria managed things more

[144] *Conf.* X, 33.

satisfactorily, according to what I often recall having heard about him: he had the singer sing the psalm with so little variation in pitch that it resembled speech rather than song."[145] Unfortunate congregation, Your Grace. Should not art be a divine service? And shouldn't divine service also be an art?

You have stopped loving, Aurel. As you have also stopped enjoying food, stopped smelling the flowers, and stopped listening too much to psalm singing. Then you write: "Now I have yet to speak again of the sensual lust of my eyes . . . The eyes love beautiful, changing forms and brilliant, fine colors. But these shall not possess my soul.

[145] Ibid.

That is for God to have. It is true that he created everything exceedingly well, but he, not the creation, is my good." Then it is as if you give a deep sigh as you say that the light of the body "has an alluring, perilous sweetness, which enhances life for those who love this world blindly." And you continue: "So inestimably much human beings have done to augment the temptations of the eyes, through various types of art and craft: with clothes and shoes, cups and vessels of all kinds, paintings and different kinds of art. And in this they more than exceed what is a necessary and reasonable need and what holds religious value. Indeed, outwardly they chase after what they create, and inwardly they desert him who created them, and thus annihilate their dis-

tinctive quality as created beings."[146] I
wonder if it is not precisely our quality as
created beings that enables us to rejoice in
God's work of creation, Your Grace. Again
I want to remind you that it is never too
late to follow the example of King Oedipus.[147]

You seem to round the whole thing off by
warning against the temptations invited by
human curiosity: "It does not wish to take
its pleasure in the flesh, but with the aid of
the flesh it wants to gain experience, through
the same bodily senses. And so it decks itself
out with names like understanding and
knowledge. This desire is an urge for knowl-

146 *Conf.* X, 34.

147 See footnote 40.

edge." [148] This is how you write, Aurel, you who were once appointed to the post of imperial rhetorician in Milano. If only you had kept quiet, you could have gone on passing as a philosopher![149]

Moreover, you warn against allowing the mind to be captivated by the course of the stars—or by a dog running after a hare. And you deal with the question in a concrete way, as if to elaborate on how natural it is

---

[148] *Conf.* X, 35.

[149] *Si tacuisses, philosophus mansisses* (If you had only kept quiet, one might have gone on believing you were wise). In my view, this is Floria's most remarkable formulation. The expression is known from *The Consolations of Philosophy* by Boethius (c. 480–524)—i.e., about a hundred years after Floria's letter. To me this is a powerful indication that Boethius—directly or indirectly—must have known Floria's letter, at least in part. Boethius was very familiar with Augustine's writings. It is surely not improbable that he was also familiar with the *Codex Floriae*. At least a few adages from Floria's letter may have reached him.

to be diverted by what the eyes see. You write: "Often when I sit at home I eagerly watch a lizard catching flies, or a spider spinning its thread around flies to entrap them in its net. Insignificant creatures, to be sure. But doesn't it come to the same thing? From such sights I turn to praising you, who in a wonderful way create and order all things. But it was not that which captured my attention from the start. One thing is to rise swiftly, another is not to fall at all."[150]

I myself come to think of Icarus.[151] At first he rose swiftly, but then he crashed. He had

---

[150] *Conf.* X, 35.

[151] From Greek mythology: Daedalus made wings out of birds' feathers and beeswax so that he and his son Icarus could fly and so escape from Crete. Daedalus warned Icarus not to fly too near the sun, which would melt the wax. But the arrogant Icarus disregarded his father's warning and flew so close that the sun burned his wings and Icarus crashed into the sea.

forgotten that he was only a human being. If you think there is a better comparison, I could also remind you of what happened to the people of Babylon after they had tried to build a tower so high that it reached right into heaven.

I write as sincerely as you, Your Grace, and the letter will not blush.[152] I think you must be exhausted after all you have been through, really exhausted. You do not hide the fact, either. If only you could now give me—and thus the physical world—a few hours more of your life on earth. Go out, Aurel! Go out and lie down beneath a fig tree. Open your senses—if only for this very last time. For my sake, Aurel, and for everything we two once gave each other. Breathe, listen to bird-

---

[152] *Epistula non erubescit*, Cicero.

song, look up at the vault of the sky[153] and draw all the odors to yourself. This is the world, Aurel, and it is here now. Here, now. You have been in the labyrinth of the theologians and the Platonists. But no longer. Now you have come back to the world again, to our human home.

The world is so big, and we know so little about it. And life is far too short. Do you remember you could say something similar when you read Cicero?

Perhaps there is no God who bargains with our poor souls. Or perhaps there is a loving God who has created us for the world so that we shall live here. Oh, Aurel, if you are lying out there beneath a fig tree—I think you're

[153] Floria writes: "Look up at Jupiter," that is, Father Jove, the god of heaven. Thus "under heaven" can stand for *sub Iove* (under Jove), for instance in Horace.

holding a fig in one hand—then I would surely come and kiss you on your all-too-worn brow. I would try to chew up that fearfully wearing word "abstinence." For still—yes, still—that word lies like a heavy burden on your mind. The only thing that might possibly have released you would have been my embrace. Why does Carthage have to be so far from Hippo Regius?

I shall see to it that you receive this letter, and I beg you to read it. But I don't hold out any hope that the words I write will truly reach you. Thus I have spilt my oil and my efforts.[154]

---

[154] Floria plays on some words by Plautus: *Oleum et operam perdidi* (I have spilt my oil and my efforts). The words are ascribed to a girl who has tried in vain to achieve success with the other sex.

I am beset with fear, Aurel. I am afraid of what the men of the church may one day do to women like me. Not just because we are women—as God has created us women. But because we tempt you who are men—as God has created you men. You think God loves eunuchs and castrati above those men who love women. Then be cautious how you praise God's work of creation, for God did not create man to castrate himself.

I cannot forget what happened in Roma, and I no longer think of myself. For really it was not I upon whom you unleashed your rage that day. It was Eve, Your Grace, the woman. And he who wrongs one, threatens many.[155]

---

[155] Cf. Syrus: *Multis minatur, qui uni facit iniuriam.*

I shiver, for I fear the day will come when women like me will be done away with by the men of the universal church. And why will they be done away with, Your Grace? Because they remind you that you have denied your own soul and gifts. And for whom? For a God, you all say, for him who created a heaven above you and also an earth which actually holds women who bring you into the world.

If God exists, may he forgive all of you. But perhaps you will be judged one day for all the joys of life you have turned your backs on. You renounce the love between man and woman. It may perhaps be forgiven. But you do it in the name of God.

Life is short, and we know far too little. But if it was at your behest that your confessions were given me to read here in Carthage, the answer is no. I shall not allow myself to be baptized, Your Grace. It is not God I fear. I feel that I live with him already, and was it not he who created me, after all? Nor is it the Nazarene who holds me back. He probably really was a man of God. And was he not also fair to women? It is the theologians I fear. May the God of the Nazarene forgive you for all the tenderness and all the love you proscribed.

I have spoken and I have unburdened my soul.[156] And now, Your Grace, now is the time for drinking![157] I am sitting beneath our

---

[156] *Dixi et salvavi animam meam.*

[157] *Nune est bibendum,* Horace.

old fig tree in Carthage. It is blooming[158] for the third time this year. But it bears no fruit.[159]

Farewell![160]

---

[158] *Floret* (from *floreo*, "to bloom, flower"). I would think Floria is again playing on her own name. For that matter, the name *Floria* must be derived from *flos, floris* (flower). Cf. *Flora*, goddess of flowers.

About a dozen miles beyond Ostia lie the ruins of an old Augustinian monastery (San Agostino). The monastery was built in the Middle Ages on the bank of the River Fiora (Floria) where it empties into the sea. In my opinion, this is surely a sign that a Floria tradition must have existed some way into the medieval period.

[159] *Fructum*, from *fructus*, which can also mean "use," "reward," or "profit." But Floria has also read the four gospels. Can she have had the parables of the fig tree in mind? (see Matthew 21:18–22 and Luke 13:6–9).

[160] *Vale!* Conventional leave-taking in letters.

I am left with many questions. Did Floria send her letter to Aurel? Or did she lack the courage in the end? There is a suggestion of that in the letter. She writes that she is afraid of what the men of the church might one day do to women like her.

As some of the notes indicate, I feel fairly convinced that the letter really was sent to the Bishop of Hippo Regius. One possibility is that it has lived a more or less hidden life throughout the history of the Roman Catholic church. Even if it has been handed down in several copies, the letter need not have been known to many people. And, naturally, the original parchment may also have remained concealed—intentionally or unintentionally—until it suddenly turned up in the sixteenth century. But what happened after that?

Perhaps my copy of the Codex Floriae lay in a monastery library until it was recently found and then sold to the little antiquarian bookshop in Buenos Aires. The proprietor said something about protecting his clients. Even a priest—or a nun, for that matter—can find himself—or herself—in circumstances leading to pecuniary necessity.

As regards the actual delivery of the letter,

I can visualize another possibility. Whether or not Augustine received it from Floria, the old parchment could have been found by the Arabs when they invaded North Africa in the seventh century. They may then have taken it with them to Spain, where it was preserved for many centuries before being rediscovered and carried to South America by the conquistadores.

Does the old parchment still exist? Perhaps. But I am more interested in other questions: How did Augustine react to the letter from his onetime lover? What did he do with it? And what did he do about Floria?

It is unlikely that we shall ever know for certain whether Augustine received Floria's letter. Although as recently as a few years ago, a previously unknown Augustine letter

was found (Peter Brown, The Body and Society [New York: Columbia University
Press, 1988], p. 397).

And, indeed, it was incredibly naive of me
not to ask the Vatican Library for a receipt
at least!

—Jostein Gaarder

Oslo

August 8, 1996